D0234721

The Case of the
VANISHING
GRANNY

The Case of the
VANISHING
GRANNY

ALEXANDER McCALL SMITH

With illustrations by Sam Usher

Conkers

First published in 2019 in Great Britain by
Barrington Stoke Ltd
18 Walker Street, Edinburgh, EH3 7LP

www.barringtonstoke.co.uk

Text © 2019 Alexander McCall Smith
Illustrations © 2019 Sam Usher

The moral right of Alexander McCall Smith and Sam Usher
to be identified as the author and illustrator of this work has
been asserted in accordance with the Copyright, Designs
and Patents Act, 1988

A CIP catalogue record for this book is available
from the British Library upon request

ISBN: 978-1-78112-857-2

Printed and bound in Great Britain by CPI Group (UK) Ltd, Croydon, CR0 4YY

For Ivy Rose

Contents

CHAPTER 1

Meet the Shortbreads

Have you ever wondered what it would be like to live in a circus? Most people visit a circus for the show, stay there until it is finished, and then go home again. But some people – circus people – live there. They go to sleep in their circus caravans and when they wake up they have their breakfast with the circus all around them. If you ask them whether they enjoy it, don't be surprised if they say something like, "This is by far the best life there is – there's nothing to beat living in a circus."

This is the story of three children who lived in a circus. Their names were Billy, who was the oldest, his sister, Fern, who was the one in the middle, and Joe, who was the youngest. Their father and mother were called Henry and Doris Shortbread, and the circus was called "Shortbreads' Great, Amazing and Wonderful Circus". They were a very happy family, not only because they all liked one another a great deal, but also because they all enjoyed what they did.

"I love being the ringmaster of my circus," said Henry Shortbread. "I love getting dressed up in my red coat and top hat. I love every moment of it."

Doris Shortbread agreed with her husband. "I love being part of the circus too," she said. "I love selling the tickets in

the booth and counting up the money at the end. I love seeing the smiles on people's faces as they leave after the show. I love all that – I really do."

"We love the circus too," said Billy.

"Yes," said Fern. "We do."

"And me too," said Joe. "Don't forget about me. I'm glad I was born a circus boy."

There were many other people who worked in the Shortbreads' Circus, and they all lived in caravans that travelled with the circus as it moved from town to town. The Shortbread family's caravan was the biggest of these, and it always led the others when the time came for everybody to go on the road. This caravan had three bedrooms in it. One of these was for Mr and Mrs Shortbread, one was for Fern, and the other

 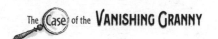

was for Billy and Joe, who shared. The boys did not mind sharing as long as they both cleared away their dirty socks and did not leave them lying on the floor.

Because they moved when the circus moved, it was hard for the Shortbread children to go to school. In fact, it was impossible. That was all right when they were very small, but as they reached an age when they had to learn to read and write, something had to be done to find a teacher.

Fortunately, Mr Birdcage, a clown who worked in the circus, had been a teacher before he became a clown.

"I always wanted to be a clown," he explained. "I started off being a teacher, but when I discovered that I was rather good at being a clown, I decided to make the change. And I did, and here I am."

Mr and Mrs Shortbread asked Mr Birdcage whether he would mind teaching their children all the things they needed to learn.

"I would be delighted to do that," said Mr Birdcage.

"You can have a special caravan as their classroom," suggested Mr Shortbread.

"That will be perfect," said Mr Birdcage.

And so that was how the children went to school – to their own school, in its special caravan, with a clown as their teacher. What could be more fun than that?

Circuses used to keep wild animals and train them to do tricks. Some even used to have lions, which they would lock in cages with strong bars. The lions would come into the ring and be made to jump through hoops and sit on upturned barrels. They would snarl at the lion tamers who would

7

make them do all this, and they were often very unhappy. So, it was decided that in future there would be no wild animals like that in circuses, because it was too cruel. Would you like to be kept in a cage and made to jump through hoops? No? Neither would I, and so you and I both agree that wild animals should not be kept in circuses.

This does not mean that dogs and horses should not be part of a circus. These animals are used to living with people and can be perfectly happy putting on a show. The Shortbreads' Circus had three very beautiful dancing horses, as well as a popular dog act. Dogs love showing off, and these dogs always looked forward to their part in the show.

There was also a cat. This cat, whose name was Leo, belonged to the Shortbread family and lived in their caravan. He was a strange-looking cat who often caused people to stop and stare when they saw him.

"There's something odd about that cat," somebody said. "Look at his fur and how long it is around his head – rather like a lion's mane. And look at his handsome long tail and his big claws ..."

"He looks rather like a tiny lion," somebody else observed.

Leo did not have a job in the circus, but he loved to wander into the tent – the big top, as it was called – when the show was in progress. Then, before anybody could stop him, he would leap into the ring and pretend to be a circus lion, roaring at the top of his voice – not that he could really roar – and making everybody laugh.

"So, this circus has a lion after all," one person said. "They have a very tiny lion."

"But that's just a cat," said another. "A cat who thinks he's a lion!"

Billy would usually retrieve Leo from the ring and take him back to their caravan.

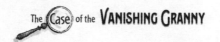

"You stay there," he said, and Leo would open his mouth to roar. But all that ever came out was a mew, and that was not enough to frighten anybody. So, Leo would just curl up on his favourite chair and dream about what it would be like to be a real lion, with a real roar and with big teeth that would scare everybody the moment he opened his mouth. Cats dream about that sort of thing, and it must be a bit disappointing for them when they wake up and discover they are still cats. But Leo, like everybody in the circus, was happy, and so he would not worry too much about all that.

CHAPTER 2

Life in the circus

Billy, Fern and Joe all had jobs in the circus. There are always plenty of things that need to be done in a circus, and if the circus belongs to your parents, then you will usually be expected to help out.

The most important task, of course, was putting up the big top. That involved pulling ropes, driving stakes into the ground and heaving

on large folds of canvas. Once that was done,
the seating stands had to be bolted together,
the lights connected and the popcorn machines
cleaned and made ready for action. There was no
shortage of things for the children to do, and they
performed all these tasks cheerfully and without
complaint.

And the work was not finished once the tent
was ready for the audience. That was the point
at which the children changed into their circus
outfits and prepared themselves for the show.
Each of the children had an act to take part in,
and their names were there on the programme,

alongside those of all the big circus stars.

Because he had such a good head for heights, Billy was part of the trapeze act. This was called "Ruffy Ruffino and His High Fliers", and it was led by Mr Ruffino and his daughter, Angela, who were billed as "Two of the world's greatest artists of the

swinging trapeze". But the programme always said: "Also starring Flying Billy Shortbread, up-and-coming master of the high swing!"

15

Fern, being such a good acrobat, had her own show, "The Elastic Bouncing Girl", which always came between the arrival of the performing dogs and the dancing horse act.

Fern would run into the ring to a roll of drums and then turn cartwheels so fast and so perfectly that most people in the audience would simply hold their breath until she stopped. After this, she would turn several somersaults, jump backwards through a hoop and finally leave the ring walking upside down on her hands. The applause was always long and loud.

Then there was Joe, whose act was called

"Young Joe Shortbread and His Clever Dogs". There were ten of these dogs, all the same breed – West Highland Terriers – with pure white coats, dark black eyes like tiny currants and pointy ears that twitched with excitement when their turn came to perform. These dogs did all sorts of tricks.

They caught balls, ran up and down see-saws and, in a grand finale at the end of their show, barked out tunes suggested by the audience. Everybody loved them and clapped long and loud when the dogs were given their reward of meaty biscuits.

So it was a busy life that the three children led, but all these things that have just been mentioned were not the end of the story. There was something else that Billy, Fern and Joe did that not so many people knew about. They solved mysteries.

That all started one day when Mr Birdcage was giving them a lesson on famous books. He had mentioned a book called *Oliver Twist*, which was all about the adventures

of a boy called Oliver in
Victorian London. Then
he mentioned William
Shakespeare, who

wrote a lot of plays. *Romeo and Juliet* was one
of his favourites, Mr Birdcage said. And then
there were books about a famous detective called
Sherlock Holmes.

Fern liked the name. "What did he do, this
Sherlock person?" she asked.

"Sherlock Holmes was his full name," said
Mr Birdcage. "People came to see him if they
needed to understand something strange that
had happened. He was very good at solving
mysteries."

"So, if you lost something," chipped in Joe,
"would Mr Holmes be able to find it?"

"Sometimes," said Mr Birdcage.

"How did he do it?" asked Billy.

"By being very observant," answered Mr Birdcage. "He looked for clues."

"Such as?" said Fern.

"Oh," began Mr Birdcage, "if somebody went to see him and he saw they had mud on their shoe, then Sherlock Holmes would say, 'I see you live in the country'. Or, if he spotted grease under your fingernails, he might say, 'I see that your bicycle chain has recently come off and you had to put it back on'. That sort of thing."

Fern smiled. "It must be wonderful to be able to help people like that."

"Well," said Mr Birdcage, "do you know something? I think you might get the chance to do that one day. You're all clever children. You know

quite a bit now that I'm teaching you, and there's something else. Do you know what that is?"

The children shook their heads.

"I think you'd like helping people," said Mr Birdcage. "Just like Sherlock Holmes."

He was right in that. Billy, Fern and Joe were kind people. They found it difficult to say no to anybody who needed help. This is a good thing, of course, but it would lead to some extraordinary adventures. And that is just what happened only a few days later: a major adventure came along.

CHAPTER 3

Granny disappears

It all started at the end of a Saturday afternoon show. The circus had just arrived in a town rather far from everywhere and would be there for some days. No circus had ever come to this town, and Mr Shortbread thought they would get good audiences. The afternoon show that day proved him right – the big top was packed with

an excited and enthusiastic crowd. But there was something odd that Fern noticed, and she mentioned this to Billy while they were watching Joe put on his dog show.

"Look over there," she said. "Look at that boy's face."

Billy looked where his sister was pointing. A boy of about his own age was sitting in a seat near the front. Others were smiling at the antics of Joe's dogs, but this boy was not. He looked miserable. When one of the dogs stood on his hind legs and did a little dance, everybody burst out laughing, but the boy's face remained sad.

Billy was puzzled. Why would somebody come to the circus if they were determined not to enjoy themselves? And why did he seem to be all alone when everybody else had friends or family around them? It seemed odd to Billy, and rather sad too.

"He doesn't look happy," Billy said to his sister.

"No," agreed Fern. "I feel really sorry for him, don't you?"

Billy nodded. "Perhaps he'll cheer up later in the show," he said.

Fern hoped that this would happen, but the poor boy appeared so sunk in misery that she thought it unlikely. But then Joe's dog act came to an end, and Fern and Billy had things to do. The two of them put the sight of the unhappy boy out of their minds and got on with the task of helping Joe to get his dogs back into the caravan that served as their mobile kennel. The dogs were always excited after a show, and they barked happily, licking any human hand, leg or even face that came within licking distance.

After the rest of the acts were over, the circus band played the tune it always played as

25

the crowd filed out of the tent. While this was happening, and while Joe was still busy settling his dogs, Billy and Fern looked after the popcorn and the hot-dog stalls at the side of the tent. These were kept open after the show so that people who felt hungry could buy themselves a final treat before they left the circus grounds. Billy sold

the popcorn in two flavours – butter and extra butter – while Fern slipped the glistening sausages into the rolls that made the delicious hot dogs.

Billy was kept busy, as it was popcorn weather and people always like popcorn when there are those sorts of clouds in the sky. But after ten minutes or so, the line of people waiting

came to end – except for one last person. That last person was the boy they had spotted earlier on, sitting sadly by himself in the audience.

Billy was surprised to see him. He thought that somebody so unhappy would slink off at the end of the show, not buy himself popcorn. But then Billy thought: *Perhaps popcorn is just the thing he needs to cheer himself up.* And then another thought came to him: he would give him the popcorn for *free*, and if that did not bring a smile to the boy's face, then nothing would.

It did not work. Even as he took the free popcorn, the thanks that the boy gave Billy were so quiet and unhappy-sounding that Billy almost did not hear them.

Billy made up his mind. He would try to find out what was wrong.

"Are you all right?" he asked as he came out of the popcorn booth to stand next to the other boy. "I saw you during the show – you looked really sad."

At first the boy said nothing. He looked at Billy as if deciding whether to trust him. Then at last he said, "I'm sorry. I didn't mean to look as if I wasn't enjoying myself. It's a really good circus."

"So, you did like it?" asked Billy.

"Yes, but ..." The boy's voice trailed off.

Billy waited. After a few moments, he pointed to a bench nearby and suggested that the two of them should sit down. "I'll sit with you while you eat your popcorn," he said. He knew that sometimes people felt better if they had a friend – and perhaps that was the problem here: this boy might have no friends.

"What's your name?" Billy asked as they sat down.

"Tom," said the boy. "And ... and I'm sorry about looking so sad, but you see I *am* sad inside, and when you're sad inside it's hard to be not sad outside – if you know what I mean."

Billy assured Tom that he undestood. "At times I feel a bit sad too," he said. "Sometimes I know why – at other times I don't. I think it's quite normal to feel a bit sad sometimes."

Tom nodded. He was becoming a bit more talkative now. "You see," he began, "it's my granny."

"Is she not feeling well?" asked Billy.

Tom looked down at his popcorn. "No," he said. "She's not ill. She's disappeared."

Billy had not been expecting this.

"Disappeared?" he exclaimed. "Do you mean she's vanished? Just like that?" He had read a story once about somebody who had become invisible. One moment she was there and then the next moment nobody could see her. She had come back of course, bit by bit, starting with her toes and ending up with the top of her head, but that was just a story. Things happen in stories that never happen in real life – except sometimes, of course.

"No," answered Tom. "She didn't vanish in a puff of smoke. Yesterday, she just left. Nobody knows where she is."

"Have they looked everywhere?" asked Billy. There were plenty of places you might find your granny if she suddenly went missing. He had heard of a granny who had suddenly decided to go off on a cruise to Florida without telling anybody. Her family had no idea about this until she sent a postcard from Orlando telling them what a good time she was having. And then there was the granny who went off to France to join the Foreign Legion, which is part of the French Army, and only returned, most disappointed, when she was told that the Foreign Legion did not take grannies. These were unusual cases, of course: most grannies stayed put and could be found every day in more or less the same place.

Tom said that he had carried out a very thorough search. "Yes, I looked everywhere," he said. "I looked in all the cupboards in her room. I looked under the table. I looked in the garden. And all the neighbours looked in these places too,

just in case she had got shut in somewhere. But there was no trace of her."

"Oh dear," said Billy. This did not sound like a story that would have a happy ending. No wonder Tom looked so miserable.

"What about your parents?" asked Billy. "What did they have to say about this?"

Tom frowned. "That's the odd thing," he replied. "My parents didn't seem to be very worried. They said, 'Oh, Granny will be all right.' That was all. But how do they know that?"

Billy was surprised. "So, they're leaving it to you to find her?" he asked.

"Yes," said Tom. "And that's one of the reasons I'm so worried. I don't know where else to look."

It was at this point that Fern joined them. She sat on the other side of Tom as he told his story once more. Feeling sorry for him, Fern put her arm around his shoulder to comfort him.

"I'm so sorry," she said. "Was she a good granny?"

"The best," answered Tom.

Fern glanced at her brother. She was sure he

was thinking the same thing. "We're going to help find your granny, Tom," she said softly.

Billy did not hesitate. "Yes," he said. "We are."

It was going to be their first case, and both of them were determined that they would help their unhappy new friend. They were not sure how they were going to do it, but they were sure they would.

Tom looked at them gratefully. And then, for the first time that day, he smiled.

CHAPTER 4

They find a clue

But how were they going to help Tom? It is easy
enough to say that you are going to solve a
mystery, but a bit harder to work out how to
do it. It was late, though, and Tom had to go
home. He told them where he lived, and Billy and
Fern agreed to come to his house the following
morning. That was a Saturday, when they had no

lessons from Mr Birdcage, and so they would be free to do what they wished.

Fern thought it might be a good idea to ask Mr Birdcage for help. Billy agreed. "He knows just about everything," he said. "Surely he would know how to find a missing granny."

They spoke to him after breakfast the next day. Mr Birdcage was sitting outside his caravan, enjoying the morning sun and reading his newspaper. He listened as they told him about their conversation with Tom. Then he stroked his chin thoughtfully, as he often did when asked a difficult question.

"This won't be easy," he replied at last. "Grannies don't usually go missing for no reason at all. When they do, it's usually because somebody has made a terrible mistake."

"Such as?" asked Billy.

"Well," said Mr Birdcage. "There was a case a few years ago of a family who took their granny with them on holiday. They went off on an aeroplane to somewhere in Spain, I think. They

had a very good holiday. There was a nice beach, I believe, and restaurants and so on. All very pleasant."

"And then?" Fern asked.

"They went to the airport and boarded the plane to come home," Mr Birdcage said. "It was only when they were halfway home that one of the children asked, 'Where's Granny?' And that was when they realised they'd left her in Spain – by mistake."

Billy caught his breath. "What happened to that poor granny?" he asked.

Mr Birdcage frowned as he tried to remember. "I think it ended all right," he began. "Yes, it did, now that I come to think of it. One of the family went straight back to Spain and found her sitting on a beach eating an ice cream. She was quite disappointed to hear that the holiday was over, as she had been enjoying herself."

"I'm glad she was found," said Fern.

"Yes," said Mr Birdcage. "But Tom's granny problem sounds a bit different. This sounds as if she might have been granny-napped."

"Granny-napped?" asked Billy.

"Yes," said Mr Birdcage. "It's a sort of kidnapping. There are some very wicked people who steal grannies and then ask for money to give them back. It's a terrible thing to do."

Fern was silent as she thought of how bad this was. There were many good people in the world, she thought – in fact, most people were good at heart – but there were also some people who thought nothing of treating others very badly indeed. This made her feel sad, but at the

same time it made her all the more determined
to do what she could to help Tom.

"You need to start at the beginning," said
Mr Birdcage. "That's what Sherlock Holmes would
do. He'd find out what she liked to do. That might
give you a clue."

They thanked Mr Birdcage
for his advice and set off for Tom's
house. They did not take Joe with
them, as he was training some
new puppies to be circus dogs and
was busy that morning. They were also worried
about taking their younger brother on what could
be a dangerous mission. So they told him where
they were going but suggested that he stay with
his dogs. "We'll tell you all about it," Fern said.
"Once we've found Tom's granny."

They did not know, of course, that Joe – and his dogs – would be more involved in this mystery than they could imagine. But we often do not know about things that are going to happen until they happen – and this was one such case.

At Tom's house, they were shown the chair where his granny normally sat. Then he showed them her room at the back of the house, with its bookcase, its cupboard and its shelf where she kept many of her day-to-day things.

"Those are her spare glasses," said Tom, pointing to a pair of spectacles on the shelf. "And that's her purse."

Billy frowned. "Her purse?"

"Yes. She always has it with her. She keeps

change in it to buy the newspaper and cups of
coffee and so on."

Tom saw that Billy was staring at him. "Is
there anything wrong?" he asked.

"You said that she always has her purse with
her," said Billy.

"Yes ..." Tom was thinking hard. "But ..."

"So why is it still here?" Billy continued.

Tom was quiet. "Yes," he said. "I see what you mean. If she normally takes it with her and it's still here, that might mean that she left in a hurry. Or ..."

Billy could see that Tom was worried. He didn't want to make him feel worse, but if he was going to help his new friend he felt he had to tell him about Mr Birdcage's theory that Tom's granny might have been kidnapped.

"Granny-napped!" Tom exclaimed when Billy finished speaking. "Oh dear," he said. "Now I'm really worried. What are we going to do?"

Billy glanced at Fern. He was not entirely sure, but he remembered Mr Birdcage's advice about finding out what Tom's granny liked to do.

He turned to Tom. "We need to know more about your granny," he said. "What does she like?"

"Chocolate," said Tom without hesitation.

"Most grannies like chocolate," observed Fern.

"Yes," Tom said. "But mine *really* likes chocolate. She loves it. Especially violet creams."

Fern asked about violet creams.

"They're a special sort of chocolate," Tom explained. "They taste of ... well, they taste of violets, I suppose. They're a bit purple inside, you see."

Billy had an idea. "Where does she get these violet creams?" he asked.

Tom said that there was a chocolate shop in the town. His granny went there regularly, he said. Then she would come back with a bag of violet creams that would last her a couple of days before she returned for more.

"Do you think she went to the chocolate shop on the day she vanished?" asked Billy.

Tom scratched his head. "I saw her that morning," he said. "She didn't say anything about going to the shops, but ..." He paused. Then his eyes opened wide. "Since you ask, now I remember. She said that she had run out of violet creams. I didn't pay much attention to that, as she was always running out of violet creams."

"Right," said Billy. "We know what to do next. Can you show us where the chocolate shop is, Tom?"

Tom nodded.

"Then that's where we must go," said Billy. And then he added, "Without delay."

It was a clue. It might not be the biggest clue, but at least it was a small clue, and even small clues have to be looked at very carefully indeed.

CHAPTER 5

At the chocolate shop

Tom showed Billy and Fern the way to the chocolate shop. It was no more than half an hour's walk, and during this time they told their new friend about their life in the circus.

"You're lucky," said Tom wistfully. "Living in a caravan must be fun – waking up in a different place every day, eating round a campfire, swinging on a trapeze and so on ..."

Billy replied that people got used to it. "It's normal life for us," he said. "And I sometimes think what fun it must be to live in an ordinary house. Waking up in the same place every day, eating round a table in the kitchen, keeping your feet on the ground rather than swinging about in mid-air ..."

They all laughed.

"Yes," mused Tom. "I suppose that other people's lives can often seem more exciting than our own."

"I'd like to work in a chocolate shop," Fern chipped in. "Eating as many chocolates as you like all day. Imagine that." She closed her eyes in pleasure. It was the most wonderful thought.

Billy was not so sure. "You'd make yourself

sick," he said. "Chocolates are delicious, but you can't eat them all day."

Fern nodded – perhaps a little bit sadly. "Maybe," she said. "But still ..."

"I bet my granny would like it," said Tom. "Especially if they were violet creams."

Nobody thought very much about what Tom said, although later they were to remember it. But now they were just around the corner from the chocolate shop, and in a minute or two it came into sight.

"That's it," said Tom, and he pointed to a large shop. It was painted bright red and had a prominent sign across its front. This said "Fudges' Fantastic Chocolates" and just beneath it was a picture of several delicious-looking chocolates.

"That one's a Walnut Whipple," said Tom,

pointing to one of the pictures. "And that one on the right is a Raspberry Surprise."

Fern's mouth was beginning to water. "I can just imagine what they taste like," she said dreamily.

Standing outside the shop, the three children

peered through the window at the display of chocolates.

"I never knew there were so many different kinds," said Billy, his nose pressed up against the glass of the shop window. "Just look at them."

"Which ones are the violet creams?" asked Fern.

Tom ran his eyes over the display. There were so many different sorts of chocolate that it took him some time, but eventually he found them.

"That tray over there," he said. "Look."

The violet creams were set out on a large tray. There were at least a hundred of them, Billy decided, and they looked delicious. Putting his hand in his pocket, he felt the couple of coins he had brought with him. He did not know how much violet creams cost, but he was sure that he would have enough money to buy at least one of the tempting-looking chocolates.

"Let's go inside," Tom suggested. "We can speak to Mr and Mrs Fudge."

Billy asked who they were, and Tom explained. "It's their shop," he said. "I don't know them, but my granny says they're very friendly. They'll tell us if they've seen her."

As they went inside, Fern sniffed at the air. It smelled of vanilla and strawberry and

marzipan. It smelled of nuts and raisins and molten toffee. But most of all it smelled of chocolate – that delicious, unmistakeable, mouth-watering smell of cocoa beans that have been dried and boiled and roasted, then stirred and pounded until they become that wonderful, unbeatable, heavenly thing – chocolate!

There were a few other customers in the shop when they went in. Mr Fudge was helping them to select chocolates from a large tray of assorted flavours. Fern, Billy and Tom gazed at the cabinets. There was a bewildering selection of chocolates, and they wondered how on earth anybody could choose.

"It's unbelievable," whispered Fern. "So many …" Her voice trailed away. Billy looked at her. Something had attracted her attention.

Now she nudged Billy. "There," she said. She was whispering so that only Billy and Tom could hear her. "Look over there."

Mrs Fudge had appeared from a door that led into the back of the shop. She was carrying a tray of what looked like freshly made chocolates. It was not this tray that interested Fern but the glimpse she had of the room beyond.

Billy and Tom followed her gaze, and in the few seconds that the door into the back was open they saw something that made them catch their breath.

"Did you see that?" hissed Tom.

They had all seen the same thing. Although it was dark at the back and the door was not fully open, they had seen the figure of what looked like a little old lady.

"My granny!" Tom exclaimed under his breath.

"Are you sure?" asked Billy, his heart racing with excitement.

Tom nodded. "I'd recognise my granny anywhere," he said. "You don't get that sort of thing wrong. You always know your own granny!"

The door into the back now slammed shut. Mrs Fudge put down the tray she was carrying and looked over towards the three children.

"Ask her," Fern whispered to Tom. "Just ask to speak to your granny."

They approached the counter. Mrs Fudge, who was not a tall person, looked up at them. "Yes?" she asked, smiling in a friendly way. "What can I do for you?"

Billy glanced at Tom. The other boy had

opened his mouth to speak but seemed to have been struck dumb. He was too nervous to speak, Billy thought.

Billy made a decision. If Tom was unable to say anything, then he would speak for him. "This boy," he said, pointing to Tom, "wants to speak to his granny."

Mrs Fudge became flustered. After a few moments of hesitation, she said, "There are no grannies here."

That was too much for Tom to bear. "But I've just seen her," he blurted out. "I saw her back there." He pointed in the direction of the door that led to the back room.

Mrs Fudge smiled. "Then you're mistaken, young man," she said. "That's the chocolate workshop. You won't find any grannies in there.

Now, if you'd like to choose some chocolates, I can put them in a bag for you."

"But ..." Tom began. He did not finish. A discouraging look from Mrs Fudge was enough to tell him that the discussion was at an end.

"I'm very busy," she said sternly. "So you children should just make up your minds. I haven't got all day, you know."

Mrs Fudge seemed anxious to get rid of them. She had been friendly at the beginning, but now she seemed worried. Had something changed?

Billy bit his lip. "We don't want any chocolates, thank you," he said firmly. And then, turning on his heel, he led the other two out of the shop. Tom cast a backwards glance as he left. He saw Mrs Fudge staring at him. He saw the door that led to the workshop move slightly. But that was all.

CHAPTER 6

Billy makes a plan

Once outside, they walked a short way down the street before anybody said anything.

"I'm sure it was her," said Tom bitterly. "I don't know why Mrs Fudge should be lying. It is her – it just is!"

Billy agreed with him. "I think something's wrong," he said. "It was as if Mrs Fudge had something to hide."

"Your granny," Fern said. "Maybe she's hiding your granny. But what should we do?"

"We could go home and tell everybody about it," suggested Tom. "Then they could tell the police and they'd come and look for her."

Billy thought about this. What Tom had proposed was a sensible thing to do, but then he thought of a reason why it might not be a good idea. "That would take time," he said. "And while we were off telling everybody, the Fudges could move your granny somewhere else."

"Yes," said Fern. "That's a good point."

"What we need to do, then," Billy continued, "is rescue her."

He waited for their reaction. A rescue would not be easy, but he thought they could at least try.

Tom needed no persuading. "Yes," he said. "We must rescue her."

Fern hesitated. It was all very well talking about rescuing people, but what exactly did that involve? "It won't be easy," she said at last.

Billy looked about him. There was a small lane beside the chocolate shop. This went along the side of the building and then disappeared into a yard at the back. "We can follow that lane," he said. "There may be another way into the building. There might be windows, or even a door that's been left unlocked."

Tom agreed and, despite her worries, so did Fern.

Making sure that nobody could see them, the three children followed the narrow lane down the side of the chocolate shop. They saw that there was a chimney at the back of the building. A wisp of white smoke, mixed with steam, rose from it up into the sky. This wafted down towards them and carried with it the smell of chocolate.

"That must be from the workshop," said Tom.

Now they were approaching a window. Unlike most windows, this was high up in the wall – too high to be looked through if you were standing in the lane.

Billy cast his eyes about for something to climb up on. A large box would have helped – or even a ladder – but ladders are never around when you need them. There was nothing.

"If only we could see through that," said Tom wistfully. "We might be able to signal to my granny inside."

Billy looked up at the window. "I could try to stand on your shoulders, Tom," he said.

Tom looked doubtful. "Would that make you high enough?" he asked.

"We could try," answered Billy.

Tom bent down in order to make it possible for his friend to get on his shoulders. Then he stood up – or tried to stand up – but did not manage to straighten out. Billy swayed for a moment, desperately attempting to get his balance, and then tumbled off. "That won't work," he said as he picked himself up off the ground.

Then Fern had an idea. What was the use, she thought, of being an acrobat if you can't jump up high when you need to? If she took a long enough run and used her brother as a springboard, then she might be able to leap high enough to see through the window. She suggested this to Billy, who readily agreed. He would kneel down below the window. His sister would run towards him, jump onto his two linked hands, and he would give her a heave up as high as he could

manage. She was very good
at flying through the air in the
circus ring, and he could see
no reason why she should not do
that now.

Their plan worked perfectly. As
Tom watched, his heart in his mouth,
Fern took a run towards her brother.
Then, with her right foot supported
in his outstretched hands, Billy
pushed upwards, sending his
sister soaring towards the
window. She reached a point
that was just high enough
for her to take a peek
through the window
before she plummeted

back towards the ground, landing gracefully on her two feet.

"Did you see anything?" Tom asked anxiously.

Fern nodded. "Yes," she said.

They waited for her to tell them.

"Is your granny a lady of about average height with her hair done up on her head like this?" asked Fern, showing how hair can be held up in a bun.

Tom nodded.

"And with little round spectacles?" Fern went on.

Again, Tom nodded.

"Then I saw her," said Fern.

It was exciting news. But seeing Tom's granny was not the same thing as rescuing her, and they still needed a plan as to how to do that.

Billy was looking around. There was a door at the back of the building. He crept over to try it, but when he turned the handle he found that it was locked, just as he had expected.

He looked up. There was another window, but that was higher than the one through which Fern had looked, and anyway it was closed. Then his attention was caught by something more promising. On the side of the roof was a skylight. This was wide open, and if they could get up there they could perhaps climb through it. Then they could find Tom's granny and bundle her out of the back door – as long as the key was in the lock, which he hoped it was.

Billy explained his plan to the others.

"It's a good idea," said Fern. She wanted

to be encouraging, but there was an obvious problem. "But how do we get up to the skylight in the first place?"

Billy smiled. "Do you see that tree over there?" he said, pointing to a tree growing alongside the building.

Fern immediately knew what her brother was thinking. "You're going to swing on a branch?" she asked.

Billy nodded. What was the use of being a trapeze artist if you could not swing on a high branch to get into a building to save somebody's granny?

Tom's eyes were wide with admiration. He felt very lucky indeed to have found such exciting new friends, but he supposed that was what happened if you met people who worked in a circus. They could do these remarkable things.

"But what about us?" Tom asked. "Do we have to climb up there and swing on that branch too?"

"Yes," said Billy. "But don't worry – I'll show you how it's done."

Tom swallowed hard. "Are you sure?" he asked.

Billy smiled. "Just don't look down," he said. "That's rule number one for trapeze artists. Don't look down."

CHAPTER 7

Through the skylight

Fern and Tom held their breath as Billy shinned his way up the tree trunk. Tom thought it looked hard, but of course Fern knew that it was nothing to her brother, who was used to climbing even higher. Each night at the circus Billy climbed hand-over-hand up the dangling rope-ladder that led to the trapeze platform hanging in the tent-top above the heads of the audience. This was much easier than that.

Once Billy was safely perched on a branch, he signalled for Fern to follow him up. She was much slower, of course, but eventually made it and seated herself on the branch next to Billy, her legs dangling downwards. Now it was Tom's turn, and he too was soon on the branch next to Billy and Fern, shaking a bit but determined not to look down.

"Right," said Billy. "Now that we all have our breath back, I'm going to show you how to do the next bit."

Fern and Tom watched as he edged his way along the branch. Then, while still seated, he reached up for another branch, directly above his head, gripped it firmly and launched himself into the air.

Tom gasped in fear. He hardly dared watch as the branch bent under Billy's weight. But then the branch straightened out again, like a spring that had been released, swinging Billy out over the gap between the tree and the roof. Once he was over the roof, he let go and dropped a few feet down onto the tiles below. "You see," he called out to them. "Easy, isn't it? Just do as I did."

"You go first," Fern said to Tom. "I don't mind being last."

"No," said Tom politely. "Please go first yourself."

From his place on the roof, Billy called out, "Come on, you two! There's no time to waste."

Tom drew a deep breath as he made his way to the end of the branch. He reached up, took hold of the other branch and launched himself into the

empty air. It took every last ounce of his courage to do this, and he almost drew back at the last moment. But now it was too late. He was flying through the air and there was nothing beneath his feet – and certainly no safety net of the sort they had at the circus.

For a moment or two, as the branch sagged under his weight, Tom imagined that it would snap and he would find himself plummeting to the ground. But that did not happen. Just as Billy had so effortlessly done, he found himself swinging over the roof. Letting go of the branch, he landed nimbly on his feet and was grabbed by Billy's steadying hands.

"There you are," said Billy. "That wasn't so difficult, was it?"

Inspired by the safe landing of the two boys, Fern now inched herself along the branch and took hold of the temporary trapeze. She too landed safely and was soon standing by her brother and Tom, ready to clamber up the roof to where the skylight beckoned them.

Billy was there first, and he peered cautiously down into the chocolate workshop below. There was nobody to be seen directly under the skylight, but he found that they were immediately above a large pile of cocoa beans, ready to be made into chocolate. "We can jump

down into those," he whispered to his friends. "The beans will break our fall."

They agreed and watched as Billy led the way. With a quiet *plopping* sound, Billy landed in the large pile of black beans and then signalled to the others to follow him. They did not hesitate, and within a few minutes the three rescuers were standing together in the dingy light of the chocolate workshop, their ears resounding with the sound of churning machinery and their noses filled with the smell of roasting cocoa beans.

Billy, Fern and Tom looked about, waiting for their eyes to get accustomed to the dim light. They looked in front, and to their left and right. But as none of the three children looked behind them, they did not see two shadowy figures come out of the darkness and approach them silently.

So they were completely taken by surprise when they suddenly found themselves seized by these figures, bundled through a doorway and then

locked away in a side room before they had the
chance to resist.

"You stay in there!" barked a voice. "That'll
teach you to break into people's chocolate shops!"

This was followed by the sound of a lock
being decisively turned, and then by silence.

"That's it," groaned Fern. "We've been
kidnapped too!"

It took a few minutes for the shock of their
imprisonment to wear off. But once it had, and
Billy was able to think sensibly once more, he sat
down on an upturned wooden box and took stock
of their situation.

"Perhaps somebody will come to rescue us,"
said Fern. "When they see that we're not at the

circus for rehearsals, they might ..." She trailed off. She could see from Billy's expression that he thought this most unlikely.

"Did you tell anybody you were coming here?" he asked.

Fern shook her head.

"In that case," said Billy, "nobody knows where we are. And how will anybody rescue us if they don't know we're here?"

"Oh dear," said Tom. "It's not looking at all good, is it?"

CHAPTER 8

Mitzi follows the trail

Back at Shortbreads' Circus, Joe, the youngest member of the Shortbread family, had finished his puppy-training session. It had taken longer than he had expected, and he imagined that by now his brother and sister would be back from the mysterious mission they had embarked on. But they were not, and now he was looking anxiously at his watch.

Before they set off for Tom's house, Billy and Fern had told their brother where they were going. It was not all that far away, and Joe decided that he would go there now and find out what had happened. Joe, of course, never went anywhere without his performing dogs, and so he put leads onto all ten of them and set off.

The dogs were all very well behaved – as

circus dogs usually are. They were used to jumping over things and turning somersaults in the ring, and so, as they made their way along the street, they did all sorts of tricks. When they came to a rubbish bin, rather than walk around it, they would jump right over it. And if there were garden walls running alongside the road, they would leap up – still on their leads – and trot along the top of the wall, just as if they were performing on a tightrope in the circus.

When they arrived at Tom's house, Joe rang the doorbell. Nobody answered. He rang the bell once more, but again nothing happened. Then he noticed that one of the dogs, Mitzi, who was the leader of the pack, was sniffing at the ground and looking up at him. When Mitzi did that, it was usually because she had come across a familiar smell and wanted to tell him about it.

Joe knew at once what it was that Mitzi was trying to say.

"Billy?" he asked. "Fern?"

Mitzi barked excitedly and began to tug at her lead.

"Everybody follow Mitzi!" Joe said to the dogs, and straightaway the whole pack, pulling and straining at their leads, tugged Joe down the garden path. When they reached the street, the dogs picked up the scent more strongly, and soon they were all running, as fast as they could manage, along the trail picked up by Mitzi.

When they reached the chocolate shop, Mitzi hesitated. It seemed as if she was uncertain as to where to go, but Sam, one of the younger dogs, soon picked up the scent and led them to the side of the building. And that was where they stopped, right at the bottom of the tree up which the other three children had climbed. They lost the scent and sat down, sniffing at the air but puzzled as to how three people could vanish into thin air.

Of course, Joe knew otherwise. He had seen

the overhanging branch and the open skylight
on the roof. He had worked out that Fern, Billy
and Tom must be somewhere inside. And he had
also worked out that if they were inside, they
could well be needing help. But how to get that
help to them? He wracked his brains, trying to
think of ways of getting up on the roof, but no
ideas came. And then, to his astonishment, Mitzi
started to whine and scratch at something with
her front paws. She had found a hole in the wall,
an air vent, and it seemed to lead right into the
building.

Joe made up his mind. If he couldn't get into
the back of the building, then at least the dogs
might be able to do so, making their way through
the air vent. It was too small for a person but was
big enough to allow a small dog to crawl through.

So, without further delay, he unclipped the leads from the dogs' collars, allowing them to follow Mitzi, who had already disappeared into the hole.

"Find Billy!" he whispered to the dogs as they wiggled their way into the air vent. "Find Fern!"

Once the dogs had disappeared, Joe had to decide what to do. He thought about this for a few moments. There was no point in standing about outside – he would go into the shop and say that he wanted to buy some chocolates. Nobody could stop you from going into a chocolate shop, and while he was doing that, he might be able to see what had happened to the dogs – and also to Billy and Fern. Were they in danger? he wondered. Had they been locked up somewhere?

Making his way round to the front of the building, he pushed open the door and entered the shop. He liked chocolate, and for a short while he stood still, breathing in the delicious smell of the wonderful confections inside. Was that vanilla? Was that the smell of apricot? And was that other, quite delicious, smell the smell of Turkish Delight covered with a thin layer of white chocolate?

Now Mrs Fudge came up to Joe and asked him whether he knew what sort of chocolates he would like to buy.

"I haven't made up my mind yet," he said. "I'd like to look."

Mrs Fudge smiled. Her manner towards him was quite different from the way she had treated the others – not that Joe was to know that. "You take your time, dear," she said, her voice warm and friendly. "There's no hurry. Pick something you'll really like – something mouth-watering, perhaps."

Joe walked over to one of the counters and started to look at the rows of delicious-looking chocolates. But all the time he was keeping an eye on the door that led into the back of the shop, and when he saw his chance, he made for that. Mrs Fudge was busy with another customer at the time, and so she did not see him darting behind the counter and slipping through the door.

Joe found himself in a large room. Along the walls there were stacked all sorts of tubs

and other equipment that a chocolate factory needs. There was also a lot of brightly coloured wrapping paper, ribbons tied in bows for sticking on top of boxes of chocolates, and containers of various fillings – marzipan, nuts, bits of candied orange-peel and so on. If he had had the time, it

91

would have been a wonderful place to look about in. But Joe had other things to do.

At the far end of the room was another door. It was firmly closed, but when Joe went over to it, he found that he was able to push it open without too much effort. And what he saw on the other side made him gasp.

There were the dogs – all ten of them – and they were all scratching at the bottom of a large locked door. Whatever they could smell on the other side of the door was of great interest to them. Joe decided immediately that this must be where Fern, Billy and Tom were.

Crossing the floor of the room, he joined the dogs. Mitzi looked up at him expectantly and then pointed with one of her paws at the locked door.

"Do you think they're in there?" Joe asked.

Mitzi barked. That bark meant only one thing: yes. That was the way a dog would say yes. You and I might think it exactly the same sound that a dog would use to say no, but Joe knew better than that. He had trained all these dogs and he knew what they meant when they barked like that.

Joe was about to knock on the door and call out to his brother and sister when the door behind him – the one through which he had come – suddenly opened. Spinning round, he saw Mr and Mrs Fudge standing there – and they did not look at all pleased.

"What do you think you're doing, young man?" asked Mr Fudge. "Are you a chocolate thief, like those others in there?"

Joe took a deep breath. He was brave, but

the tone of Mr Fudge's voice was threatening and really rather frightening.

"I'm looking for my brother and sister," said Joe, his voice sounding very small and weak.

Mr Fudge glanced at Mrs Fudge, and she glanced back at him. Joe could tell they were not pleased.

"You can join them if you like," said Mr Fudge, his voice full of menace.

"Yes," said Mrs Fudge. "There's plenty of room where they are safely locked up."

Joe did not know what to do. The Fudges were much bigger than he was, and he did not stand a chance of getting away from them. But then, just as he was beginning to think that he was completely trapped, he saw something that caught his attention. Mr Fudge was holding a bunch of keys, all tied up with string. One of those must be for the locked door behind which the others were being kept. And when he saw that, an idea came into his mind. He was not alone in this dangerous situation – he had with him ten brave assistants, and there were only two Fudges.

Joe turned to Mitzi, who was standing close to his feet, growling softly at the Fudges.

"Over there, Mitzi!" Joe suddenly shouted, pointing to Mr Fudge and his bunch of keys. "Fetch, Mitzi, fetch!"

Circus dogs are very highly trained – and very bright. Many dogs would not have known what to do, but Mitzi did. Without waiting for a second command, she dashed forward, her hackles raised. And behind her, like soldiers following their leader, went the other nine dogs, growling and barking and making as much noise as they could.

The Fudges froze. It is not easy to run away when you are being encircled by ten excited and angry dogs. So they were not prepared for what

Mitzi did next, which was to leap up and snatch the bunch of keys in her jaws. Then, before Mr Fudge could do anything to stop her, she raced back to Joe and dropped the keys at his feet.

It was easy for Joe now. Because they were surrounded by the rest of the dogs, the Fudges could not do anything to stop Joe finding the right key and opening the heavy door behind him. And there, astonished to find themselves rescued – but very pleased nonetheless – were Fern, Billy and Tom.

"It's you!" shouted Fern. "Well done, Joe!"

"Well done, Mitzi," said Joe. "She's the one who deserves the credit."

Mitzi had more to do. There was another door, not far away, and she was scraping at this with her paws.

"She's found something," said Fern.

Billy went over to the door and tested it. It was not locked, and when he opened it he caught his breath in surprise over what he saw. There, sitting in front of a large table covered in chocolates, was Tom's granny.

She was surprised. "Well, well," she said when she saw her grandson. "What on earth are you doing here, Tom?"

"We've come to rescue you, Granny."

A look of complete surprise came over his granny's face. "Rescue me? What from?"

"From those wicked people there," said Tom. "From the granny-nappers."

This brought a loud snort from Mr Fudge. "Granny-nappers? Who are you to accuse us of being granny-nappers?" Then, turning to point at Fern and Billy, he continued, "Those children are chocolate thieves. We trapped them when they were coming in to steal our chocolate. We were going to call the police to come and collect them."

"Chocolate thieves!" burst out Billy. "We're not chocolate thieves! We're granny-rescuers."

It was obvious that there had been a big mistake somewhere, and it was Tom's granny who sorted it out. "Let's all sit down and talk about this," she said. "I think there has been a misunderstanding."

They all sat down and talked, and the story became clear. Tom's granny had not been granny-napped. She was actually very friendly with the Fudges and had asked them to help her with a special plan she had cooked up.

"Your birthday's coming up, isn't it, Tom?" she said.

Tom nodded. "In two days' time, Granny."

Tom's granny smiled. "And I know how much you like chocolate," she continued. "I thought I would make you a special chocolate cake – the very best chocolate cake ever. It would be made

of one hundred different kinds of chocolates, in the shape of a castle. It would be quite unlike any other chocolate cake in the history of the world."

Tom's jaw dropped. "Is that what you've been doing here?" he asked.

His granny nodded. "It was to be a surprise, and so I came to stay with my friends here for a few days while I worked on it. They've been helping me."

Mrs Fudge nodded. "I'm so sorry about what happened," she said. "We were trying to keep the whole thing secret. And then, when we found you inside the workshop, because it was dark we didn't recognise you. We really did think you were chocolate thieves. We're so sorry."

After this, everybody laughed. It had all been a misunderstanding. Tom's granny was perfectly safe. It was a pity that the birthday cake would no longer be a surprise, but Tom had not seen all that much of it, and so bits of it would be new to him on his birthday.

"Did my mum and dad know all about it?" asked Tom.

His granny nodded. "They were in on the secret," she said. "I had to tell them."

"Then they knew you were perfectly safe?" asked Tom.

"Yes," said his granny. "But they couldn't tell you where I was, could they? That would have ruined the surprise."

"We owe you an apology," said Mr Fudge.

"Would you accept a tray of chocolates to make up for it?"

The children agreed that this would more than make up for what had happened. "And we should say sorry to you too," said Billy. "We thought you were wicked."

"They're not wicked at all," said Tom's granny. "How could anybody who makes such delicious chocolates be wicked?"

Tom's granny went home with Tom, while Billy, Fern and Joe went back to the circus with their dogs. There they told their parents and Mr Birdcage about what had happened. He smiled.

"You did very well," Mr Birdcage said. "You found clues and you followed them up. It's not your fault you got it all wrong, because you have to get some things wrong before you get them right."

Billy thought that was very true, and he wrote it down in a notebook that he kept to record what Mr Birdcage taught them.

That night, Tom came to the circus, this time with his granny and Mr and Mrs Fudge. The Fudges were in a very good mood and brought free chocolates as a gift for all the other members of the circus. This made them very popular indeed.

And for the dogs, Tom's granny brought a bag of dog biscuits that she gave to them after the show. The dogs were pleased. They hoped that there would be more detective work for them in the future.

Two days later, Tom had a party to celebrate

his birthday. The amazing cake made out of
chocolates was on show, and everybody had the
chance to see it, photograph it and then eat a
piece. They all agreed there had never been a

cake quite like it, although they hoped that one day there would be another.

And that was the first mystery that the three circus detectives solved. There would be more, they hoped – and there were.

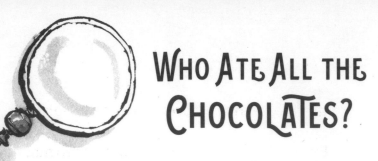

WHO ATE ALL THE CHOCOLATES?

Someone has eaten a lot of violet creams at Tom's birthday party. Using the clues on the opposite page to fill in the table, can you help Billy, Fern and Joe work out who has eaten the most chocolates?

Clues

1. Mr Fudge ate more than 2 violet creams.

2. Mrs Fudge had the fewest violet creams.

3. Tom ate an odd number of violet creams.

4. Granny ate less than Tom.

		Number of Chocolates Eaten			
		1	2	3	10
Party Guests	Tom				
	Granny				
	Mr Fudge				
	Mrs Fudge				

Answer on page 110

Fudges' Fabulous Chocolate Truffles

Mr and Mrs Fudge weren't granny-nappers after all. They were very kind people who shared their secret recipe for chocolate truffles with the Shortbread children. These truffles are so easy to make that Billy, Fern and Joe will be able to mix up a batch when they're out on the road with the circus, and you can make them at home!

Answer to WHO ATE ALL THE CHOCOLATES? on page 109: Mr Fudge (Mr Fudge ate 10 violet creams, Mrs Fudge ate 1, Tom ate 3 and Granny ate 2)

You will need

- 100g bar of dark chocolate
- 20g unsalted butter
- 100ml double cream
- An adult's help!

Method

1. Break the chocolate up into pieces in a medium-sized bowl.

2. Put the butter and cream in a saucepan and heat very gently until the butter melts and the cream starts to simmer.

3. Pour the butter and cream over the chocolate and stir together until the chocolate melts and you have a smooth mixture.

4. Let the mixture cool a little and use a teaspoon to pull over the top of the mixture to form it into small balls. This bit can get messy!

5. You can then coat your truffles by rolling them in cocoa powder, hundreds and thousands or coconut.

6. Eat and enjoy!

The Great

Clown
Conundrum

Coming to town in
Autumn 2019!

978-1-78112-880-0